KW-423-974

Contents

Introduction

'What's wrong with you?' Sheena said angrily. 'You don't talk to me. You don't talk to your father.'

Tessa is sixteen, angry and unhappy. She never wanted to come to Seagull Island with her father and Sheena, her stepmother. She enjoyed her old life in the town of Inverkeld, and she wants to go back there. And now there is a new problem – Sheena is having a baby. How can Tessa get away from Seagull Island?

On the night of a bad storm, Sheena has an accident and her baby is coming. The telephone isn't working. So Tessa forgets her problems and takes her father's boat out to sea.

Can she get to the town and find a doctor? And can she be happy again?

Elizabeth Laird was born in New Zealand. She was a teacher in Malaysia, Ethiopia and London, and she also lived in Lebanon, Iraq and Austria. Now she writes for young people, and you can read her books in many different languages. *The Earthquake* and *Karen and the Artist* are Penguin Readers, too.

Elizabeth Laird and her husband, the writer David McDowall, have two children.

Chapter 1   A Girl Alone

There was a strong wind that evening on Seagull Island. The sky was dark, and the waves were very big.

Tessa Maclean stood at the top of the cliff, high above the beach. She looked across the sea to the lights of the town.

'I hate it here,' she thought. 'I don't want to work for my father. I want to go back to Inverkeld. I was happy there.'

On the beach below, she could see a young man. It was Jim Logan, the only other young person on the island. He was there with his boat.

Jim looked up and saw Tessa. He stopped working for a minute. Tessa wanted to call to him, but she didn't.

'He never speaks to me,' she thought. 'Perhaps he doesn't like me. Nobody on this island likes me.'

Jim turned back to his boat and pulled it onto the beach.

'Tessa!' somebody called.

Tessa looked round. It was Sheena, Tessa's stepmother. She was outside the Macleans' house, on the top of the cliff.

'Tessa!' Sheena called again. 'What are you doing out here? Your father's waiting for you.'

She walked across to Tessa.

'Why do you come here every evening?' she asked Tessa. 'What are you looking at? What do you want?'

'Go away,' Tessa thought. 'I don't want *you*. You're not my mother. You don't understand me.' But she said nothing.

'Why don't you talk to me?' said Sheena.

'I want to go home to Inverkeld,' thought Tessa. 'I want my old life . . . I want my mother.'

'Why don't you want to be my friend?' asked Sheena. 'Why don't you . . . ?'

'Oh, leave me alone,' Tessa said suddenly. 'Please, can't you leave me alone?'

Then she saw Sheena's unhappy face and felt sorry for her. She wanted to say something friendly, but she couldn't.

'What's wrong with you?' Sheena said angrily. 'You don't talk to me. You don't talk to your father. You know that my baby's coming next month. I can't do much in the house. I can't work on the farm. *You* have to help your father. But you don't . . . '

Tessa's eyes opened wide. She was angry now, too.

'That's unkind!' she said. 'I *do* help you and Dad! I worked on the farm with him this morning. I worked in the house this afternoon. Can't I have a little time alone? What's wrong with that?'

She turned away from Sheena and started to run back to the farmhouse. Sheena followed her slowly. She couldn't walk fast.

Tessa opened the door of the farmhouse and went inside. A big, heavy farmer was at the table. It was Tessa's father, John Maclean.

'Where did you go?' he said. 'Where's Sheena?'

'She's coming,' Tessa said.

John Maclean looked unhappy.

'Were you unkind to her again?' he said.

Tessa said nothing. When Sheena came into the room, John Maclean looked at his wife's face.

'What's wrong now?' he said.

'Ask Tessa,' Sheena said. 'Ask your daughter.'

John Maclean looked at Tessa, but he didn't say anything. Tessa put some food on the table.

'Get me some bread,' her father told her. 'Then sit down and eat. I don't want to hear a word from you.'

Tessa sat down. She was very angry. 'He thinks I'm a child,' she thought. 'But I'm sixteen, not six.'

John Maclean started to eat.

Nobody talked. They could hear the wind outside.

'I'm going to take the boat to Inverkeld tomorrow,' John said to Sheena. 'Do you want anything?'

'You're going to Inverkeld?' Tessa said. 'Oh, Dad, please, please take me with you.'

Her father looked at her.

'No,' he said. 'You can stay here with Sheena. The baby's coming in five weeks. Stay and help her.'

Tessa stood up.

'Jim Logan's mother can come,' she said. '*She* can help Sheena. Please, Dad, I don't want to stay here. You know that. I don't want to work on the farm. I want to go back to Inverkeld. I want to find a job there.'

'Don't listen to her, John!' said Sheena.

Tessa looked at Sheena.

'I'm talking to my father,' she said. 'Not to you.'

'Don't speak to Sheena in that way!' her father shouted.

'All right,' said Tessa. 'I'll never speak to her again!'

John Maclean's face was red. He was very, very angry. He stood up suddenly and tried to catch Tessa's arm. She ran behind her chair and his hand hit the teacup. The hot tea ran off the table on to Sheena's legs. She jumped up.

'Sheena! Are you all right?' cried John.

'My legs! My dress! Oh, look, my legs!' cried Sheena.

Suddenly, Sheena sat down again in her chair. She put her hands on her stomach.

'What's wrong, dear?' John said.

'It's the baby,' said Sheena. 'I think ... '

'It's not possible,' said John. 'It's too early. It's only eight months.'

Sheena's face was white.

'Eight months or nine months, it's coming now,' she said. 'Call the air ambulance. I want the doctor, John. Now!'

Chapter 2   Emergency!

John Maclean ran to the telephone.

'Hello?' he shouted. 'Hello?'

'What's wrong, Dad?' asked Tessa.

'The telephone's not working,' her father said. 'It's the wind.'

'John! Help me! John!' Sheena called.

John Maclean put his hands over his eyes for a minute and thought.

'I'll take the boat to Inverkeld,' he said. 'I'll find the doctor and bring him back here.'

He went to the door of the farmhouse and opened it. The wind hit him in the face.

'The wind's too strong,' he said. 'I can't take the boat out in this weather.'

'You have to go, John! Go to Inverkeld and get the doctor!' cried Sheena. 'I can't . . .'

Tessa ran to her.

'I'll help you,' she said. 'You'll be all right. I'll . . .'

'Go away!' cried Sheena. 'Don't come near me!'

'I'll get Mrs Logan,' John Maclean said. 'She knows about babies.'

He went outside.

'No!' shouted Sheena. 'I don't want Mrs Logan! I want a doctor . . .'

But John Maclean wasn't there.

'Please, Sheena,' Tessa said quietly. 'You'll be all right. Mrs Logan isn't a doctor, but she works in a hospital. She can help . . .'

"Be quiet!' Sheena said. 'This is *your* fault!'

'No,' cried Tessa. 'Oh no!'

She ran to the door and went outside. It was very dark now. She fought her way through the heavy wind, down to the sea.

'I have to get a doctor,' Tessa thought. 'I'll go to Inverkeld!'

She came to her father's old boat. She jumped into it and started the engine. Then she started to undo the ropes.

Suddenly, in the dark night, somebody called her name. There was a man on the top of the cliff.

'It's Dad,' thought Tessa. 'He wants to stop me, but I'm not going to stop now.'

The ropes were wet and heavy. Tessa pulled and pulled. The man was on the beach now. When the ropes were all in the boat, Tessa turned the boat out to sea.

Suddenly, she heard a noise behind her and the man jumped into the boat. It wasn't her father. It was Jim Logan.

Chapter 3   Into the Storm

'Tessa Maclean, what are you doing?' Jim said. 'You can't take a boat out in this weather.

'I can and I will,' Tessa said.

'But the wind! It's . . . '

'Listen,' said Tessa. 'I'm going to Inverkeld. Are you coming with me? Then help me. Or are you afraid? Then jump off the boat and swim back to the beach.'

'But it's dangerous!' Jim shouted.

He put his hands on the wheel.

'Stop it!' said Tessa angrily. 'I can do it.'

A big wave hit the boat and the wheel turned in Tessa's hands. She couldn't turn it back. Jim pushed her away and pulled the wheel round.

Another wave hit them. The boat went up high and then came down again quickly. The wind was stronger away from the beach and the cliffs.

'You stupid girl,' Jim shouted angrily. 'I know you're running away! But why are you going tonight? In this weather? Why?'

'What?' said Tessa. 'Don't you know? Sheena . . . '

Another, bigger wave hit the little boat. Water started to come into the boat.

'Be careful!' shouted Jim. 'I think the boat's turning over!'

'I'm wearing the wrong shoes for a wet boat,' Tessa thought. 'I'm going to fall.'

Another wave hit them. The boat went up again, but it didn't turn over. Tessa could stand up again now. She took off her shoes.

She looked up at Jim, at his hands on the wheel.

'Hey!' she shouted. 'What are you doing?'

'I'm turning the boat round,' said Jim. 'We're going back to the island.'

'No!' said Tessa. 'I *have* to go to Inverkeld! Sheena . . .'

'Don't be . . .' began Jim.

'Listen!' shouted Tessa. 'Why don't you *listen* to me? Sheena's baby's coming and it's five weeks early. The telephone isn't working. I have to get the air ambulance.'

'What?' said Jim.

'Didn't you know?' Tessa said. 'Didn't my dad tell you?'

'He ran past me,' said Jim. 'He didn't stop and talk. He wanted to see my mother. Why didn't you tell me about Sheena before?'

'You didn't want to listen,' said Tessa. 'I'm only a stupid girl, remember? I'm running away from home in the middle of a storm? OK, I'll take you back to the island, then I'll go to Inverkeld alone.'

8

But Jim turned the boat round again. It was very difficult in the strong wind.

'I'm sorry,' he said. 'I didn't understand. I'll come to Inverkeld with you. You can't do this alone.'

Tessa closed her eyes for a minute. She wasn't angry now. She was happy. 'He can help me with the boat,' she thought.

'Thank you,' she said. 'But you don't have to come. I know it's dangerous.'

For the first time, Jim smiled.

'That's OK,' he said. 'You can't stop me. It's not going to be easy. I often go to Inverkeld by boat, but I never go at night. There are rocks between here and the town. They're under the water and we won't see them in the dark.'

'I know,' Tessa said. 'We'll have to be careful. I'll get out the life jackets.'

She opened a cupboard under the wheel and pulled out two life jackets. They put them on.

'Thank you, Jim,' she said. 'Thank you for your help.'

Chapter 4   The Lights of Inverkeld

Jim stood at the wheel. It was heavy in the storm.

'Can you take this, Tessa?' he said. 'My arms are tired.'

Tessa took the wheel. When she turned it, it felt heavier than before. She couldn't see the sky. Here, on the open sea, she could see only waves. They were dark, and as big as mountains.

Jim took the wheel again. They couldn't talk much. The noise of the wind and the waves was very loud.

The wind pushed the little boat across the water. The waves carried it up, then pulled it down and down again.

'We'll never get to Inverkeld,' thought Tessa. 'I'm going to die. Jim's going to die too. And it's all my fault.'

The boat came up again. Suddenly, through the storm, Tessa saw lights. The boat came off the top of the wave and went down again. Then it was high up on the next wave. She looked again.

'We're nearly there,' shouted Jim. 'Those are the lights of Inverkeld.'

Tessa could see the lights. But something was wrong.

'No! That's not Inverkeld!' she cried. 'Inverkeld's bigger than that. You can see hundreds of lights from Seagull Island.'

The boat went down . . . down . . . down into another big wave and up to the top of the next wave. Then, for a minute, the moon came out. Jim and Tessa could see better now. It wasn't Inverkeld in front of them. Inverkeld was a long way away to the left. The lights came from a village on the top of a cliff. And the cliff was nearer now!

'Jim!' shouted Tessa. 'The cliff! Look! We're going to hit it!'

'I know!' shouted Jim. 'I'm turning the wheel! The rocks . . . Where are the rocks?'

'I don't know,' Tessa shouted back. 'I can't see. Yes! Look! They're on our left!'

Jim tried to turn the wheel round, but the big waves pulled the boat back to the cliff.

'Help me, Tessa,' he shouted.

Tessa pulled the wheel, too.

'I think – yes, it's turning,' said Jim.

Slowly, the boat turned away from the cliff. Tessa shut her eyes for a minute.

'Thank you,' she said quietly.

They couldn't see the moon now. It was dark again.

'Are you OK?' shouted Jim.

'I – yes,' said Tessa. 'Where are we?'

'I don't know,' answered Jim. 'I fish out here sometimes, but in the dark . . . '

There was a sudden noise under the boat. Then it stopped moving.

'What happened?' shouted Tessa. 'Did we hit the rocks?'

'No,' said Jim. 'We're on a sandbank. We can't move.'

Chapter 5   On the Sandbank

Jim stopped the engine. It was suddenly quieter in the boat. Out at sea the storm was bad, but the sandbank was near the cliffs. The wind was weaker here, and the waves weren't as high. Jim and Tessa could talk easily again.

'We can't do anything,' Tessa said. 'There isn't much water here. We'll never get the boat off the sandbank.'

Jim looked at his watch. 'The sea's coming in now,' he told her. 'We'll only be here for an hour.'

'An hour?' said Tessa. 'But Sheena . . . '

'We can't do anything,' said Jim. 'We can only wait.'

They said nothing for some time. Then Jim said, 'Listen, Tessa. I'm sorry.'

'Sorry? Why are you sorry?' asked Tessa.

'I said some things to you . . . I was unkind because I was angry.'

'What things?'

'I called you a stupid girl.'

'Now you know that I'm not running away,' Tessa said. 'But I don't like the island. We lived near Inverkeld, and it was my home. I was happy there. I had a lot of friends and I loved my school.'

She stopped.

'But then your mother died,' said Jim quietly.

'Yes. I was thirteen. It was – oh, it was difficult. Dad and I were alone for two years. We were good friends. But then he met Sheena, and they married. He sold our old farm, and bought the farm on Seagull Island. I wanted to get a job in Inverkeld, but Dad wanted me to live with them. "You've got a new mother now," he said. A new mother? Sheena isn't my mother! Mum was kind, and funny, and strong, and . . .'

She stopped again. Jim put his hand on her hand.

'You're crying,' he said.

'It's all right,' said Tessa. 'Mum was a – a wonderful person. Now she's dead, and I can't . . .'

'You're sad, I know,' said Jim. 'But you can't hate Seagull Island. Perhaps you're not happy with Sheena and your father, but don't hate the island!'

'Why not?' said Tessa. 'There's nothing there for me. Some animals, some old people, one or two beaches – that's all.'

'What?' said Jim. 'That's *all?* What's wrong with your eyes? Don't you see the birds in the sky? Don't you feel the clean, cold wind in your hair? There are thousands of beautiful little flowers on the cliffs. Don't you want to know their names? Don't you watch the morning sun over the sea? And don't you watch it in the evening, a ball of fire? Seagull Island's the most beautiful place in the world!'

'Jim!' said Tessa. 'Those are wonderful words. Write them down!'

Jim laughed.

'I'm not a writer. I catch fish,' he said.

'But don't you want to be with other young people?' asked Tessa. 'There isn't anybody of our age on the island.'

Jim smiled at her.

'There *weren't* any,' he said. 'But then you came.'

The boat suddenly moved.

'There's more water under the boat now,' said Jim. 'We're moving again. We'll have to be very, very careful. There are hundreds of rocks between here and Inverkeld, and the wind's very strong.'

'I'm afraid, Jim,' said Tessa.

'I am too,' said Jim. 'But we can't go back now.'

Chapter 6   Into the Sea!

Jim started the engine and turned the boat away from the sandbank. But the wind and waves were stronger than the small engine. Slowly the boat moved back to the cliffs.

'Rocks!' Tessa shouted suddenly. 'Look! In front of us!'

Jim tried to turn the wheel, but he couldn't. Tessa helped him.

But it was too late. The boat hit the rocks.

'Look, Jim! Look!' shouted Tessa. 'Water's coming into the boat!'

'We can't stay here!' shouted Jim. 'We'll have to swim!'

Tessa opened the door. Cold water hit her face. It nearly pushed her into the sea.

'I'm going to die,' she thought. *'We're* going to die.'

Another big wave hit the boat and turned it over. Jim hit his head on the boat. His eyes closed, and he fell back into the water. A second wave threw him at the boat.

The same wave took Tessa down into the cold, cold water. Water ran into her mouth and nose.

'No!' she thought. 'No!'

She kicked strongly and came up again. She wasn't dead! She looked round. Where was Jim?

The next wave pulled her up high in the sea. She could see Jim now. He was very near her, but his face was down in the water.

'Jim!' shouted Tessa.

The next wave broke over Tessa's head. Water ran into her nose and mouth again. But she was ready this time and she started to swim. She went to Jim and turned him over. His eyes were shut. She hit him with her hand.

'Open your eyes, Jim!' she shouted. 'Swim!'

Jim didn't move. Tessa took his life jacket in one hand and tried to swim. But the waves were too strong.

In front of her, she could see the rocks at the bottom of the cliff. The waves pulled the two young people their way.

'This is it!' Tessa thought. 'We're going to die now. Oh, I hope it doesn't hurt too much!'

But then she felt something under her feet. She put her feet down. She could stand.

'Jim!' she shouted. 'Where are we? Do you know this place? Oh please, Jim, say something!'

But Jim didn't speak.

Then, suddenly, the moon came out, and Tessa could see in front of her. Between the cliffs was a small beach.

'Jim!' she said. 'We're going to be all right. There's a . . . '

A big wave hit her back. Jim's life jacket fell from her hands. There was water in her eyes, and the waves pushed her off her feet. Suddenly, she was out of the sea. She was on the beach, and Jim was next to her.

He didn't open his eyes. He didn't move.

'Please,' Tessa cried. 'Don't die. Oh, Jim, don't die!'

She opened his life jacket and listened. He wasn't dead! Then suddenly, water ran out of his mouth.

'Jim!' said Tessa. 'Listen to me. You're hurt, but you're going to be all right. We're going to be all right.'

But the beach was small, and there were high cliffs behind it. She looked at the sea.

'It's coming in fast,' she thought. 'Half the beach is underwater now.'

Jim was half in and half out of the sea. Tessa stood up and began to pull him out of the water. It was difficult. He was big, and his wet clothes were heavy.

She stopped for a minute. Then, on the beach, Jim's hand moved. Tessa took it in her hand. He turned his head and his eyes opened. He said something. But he spoke very quietly, and Tessa couldn't hear him. She put her head down to his mouth.

'Where are we?'

'We're on a small beach near Inverkeld,' Tessa said. 'There's no way out of it, and the sea's coming in. Jim, I'm sorry. I'm very, very sorry.'

Jim's eyes shut again.

'Oh, please,' Tessa said, 'open your eyes.'

'I'm OK,' said Jim. 'I'm thinking. Now look up. Are there two trees at the top of the cliff?'

Tessa looked up. She could see two black trees in the weak moonlight.

'Yes,' she said.

'I think I know this beach,' said Jim. 'There *is* a way up to the top. It's not easy. You have to climb.'

'*You* can't climb,' Tessa said. 'You're hurt.'

'No, but *you* can,' said Jim. 'You'll have to be careful. The rock's wet. But I think you can do it. I know you can.'

'I don't want to leave you,' Tessa said. 'You're hurt, and the sea's coming in.'

'You *have* to do it,' Jim said, 'or we'll die. You've got half an hour. Perhaps longer. Go!'

'You'll have to get higher up the beach,' said Tessa. 'I'll help you.'

She pulled Jim up. He put one arm round her and began to walk up the beach.

'Does your head hurt?' Tessa asked.

'Yes,' Jim said. 'But I'll be OK. Go now, Tessa! We haven't got much time!'

He sat down on the beach.

'Look,' he said. 'Can you see that big rock? The climb begins there.'

Chapter 7   On the Cliffs

The moonlight wasn't strong, but Tessa could see the best places for her hands and feet on the cliff. She began to climb. She had no shoes, so it was difficult on the wet rocks. Below her, she could hear the noise of the waves. The water was high on the beach now.

'Quick,' thought Tessa. 'I have to be quick!'

Her fingers and feet hurt. But she climbed up and up.

The noise of the waves from the beach below was very loud. Tessa looked down. The beach was a long, long way below her now. Her legs felt weak, and she was afraid. She looked up the cliff. Where was the next place for her hands? There was only a small rock a long way above her.

'I'll have to jump and catch that,' she thought. 'I'll *have* to catch it, or I'll fall.'

But she couldn't move. She was afraid. Then she heard the noise of the waves again on the beach.

'Jim!' she thought. 'I have to save him! How much time have I got? Perhaps he's in the sea now!'

She jumped, and caught the rock with her hands. But now her

18

feet were in the air. She moved them slowly across the cliff. Her arms were very tired.

'I'm going to fall!' she thought. 'I'm falling!'

She shut her eyes. But then she felt a rock with her right foot and stood on it. She could go up again now. Her hands and feet hurt, but she went up and up.

When she came to the top of the cliff, she fell down on the ground. She couldn't run. She couldn't stand.

Then she heard the sea again. 'What did Jim say?' she thought. 'Half an hour?'

She got up and began to run to the lights of the village. She fell, then ran again. Near the first house there was a telephone box. She ran into it and called the emergency number.

A woman answered.

'Quick!' said Tessa. 'There's a man at the bottom of the cliff. We had an accident, and the sea's coming in. Send somebody quickly, please!'

She ran back to the cliffs. She waited for five minutes, then another five.

'Where are you? Oh, where are you?' she thought.

Then she saw a blue light. The coastguards arrived, and an ambulance. The men jumped out and looked down the cliff.

'There's somebody down there?' they said to Tessa. 'How do you know?'

'Our boat turned over in the storm,' Tessa said. 'We had to swim to the beach. I climbed up the cliff. Jim couldn't climb up, because he's . . . '

'You climbed up there in the dark?' a coastguard said. 'That's not possible!'

The men worked quickly. They went down the cliff with ropes. Tessa waited.

'He's dead,' she thought. 'I know he's dead.'

Then she heard the coastguards again. They were on ropes at

the top of the cliff. The last man had Jim in his arms.

'Is he – is he . . . ?' Tessa asked.

'He's all right,' one of the men answered. 'The water was over his legs, but he'll be fine.'

'Quick, get him into the ambulance,' said the ambulance man. He turned to Tessa. 'You can come to the hospital with him. The doctor will want to look at your feet.'

Suddenly, Tessa remembered Sheena and the baby.

'The hospital!' she said. 'Oh please, please call them on your radio! My stepmother's having a baby on Seagull Island. She's . . . '

'Seagull Island?' said the coastguard. 'You came from Seagull Island tonight? In this storm? That wasn't very clever!'

Jim heard the coastguard's words from the door of the ambulance. He smiled.

'Oh yes, it was,' he said. 'Tessa's wonderful. Tessa, you're a wonderful, wonderful girl!'

Chapter 8   A Family Again

Tessa went in the back of the ambulance with Jim. The driver used his radio.

'Can you send the air ambulance to Seagull Island?' he said. 'A woman's having a baby, and it's five weeks early.'

They arrived at the hospital quickly, and the doctors took Jim away.

'I'll come and visit you, Jim,' Tessa said.

'You don't have to,' said Jim. 'I'm not going to stay here. I want to get back to the island.'

'I'll be there,' Tessa said.

'Really?' said Jim. 'You're not going to leave?'

'Oh no,' said Tessa. 'Not now. I'm not going to leave now.'

A doctor came to Tessa.

'Are you the girl from the island?' he asked. 'Is your mother having a baby?'

'My – yes,' said Tessa. 'Yes, my mother.'

'The air ambulance is ready,' the doctor said. 'I'm going out to Seagull Island now.'

'Oh, please,' said Tessa, 'can I go with you? I want to go home.'

'I'm sorry,' the doctor said. 'The air ambulance only carries doctors.'

Tessa thought quickly.

'I'll have to go,' she said. 'You don't know the way to our house.'

The doctor smiled.

'All right,' he said. 'You win. Let's go.'

Tessa looked down from the air ambulance on to the dark sea.

'Is Dad very angry with me?' she thought. 'And Sheena – is she all right?'

They came down near the farmhouse and Tessa ran home fast. The doctor followed her more slowly.

Tessa opened the door. Her father was in the kitchen. John Maclean looked up.

'Tessa!' he said. 'Oh, my little girl! You're all right! You came back! I'm sorry. It was my fault. I . . .'

'Oh, Dad . . .' said Tessa. 'It's not important now. How's Sheena? Is she all right?'

Her father's face was sad.

'Sheena's fine,' he said. 'Mrs Logan's with her. She helped – she did everything. But the baby isn't well. We'll have to get a doctor when we can. I'm afraid . . .'

'The doctor's here, Dad,' Tessa said. 'I went to Inverkeld and I came back with the air ambulance. The doctor's coming now.'

The doctor came quickly into the farmhouse.

'Doctor?' John Maclean said. 'Oh, doctor! Please come with me.'

He took the doctor into the bedroom.

An hour later, the doctor called Tessa.

'Come and meet your little brother,' he said.

'My brother?' said Tessa. 'Is he going to be all right?'

'Yes,' the doctor said. 'He'll be all right now. You saved him, Tessa. You saved his life.'

Tessa went into the bedroom. Sheena was in bed. She looked white and tired. The baby was in her arms.

'Oh, Tessa,' said Sheena. 'I'm sorry. I was unkind to you. Your father loves you very much, and I wanted him to love me. I didn't want you here. But now . . .'

'It's OK, Sheena,' Tessa said. 'It was my fault. I was worse than you. Can I see the baby?'

'Yes,' Sheena smiled. 'He's yours, too.'

She put the baby into Tessa's arms.

'My little brother,' said Tessa. 'My dear little brother.'

She looked up at her father.

'We're a family again now, Dad,' she said happily.

ACTIVITIES

Chapters 1–4

Before you read

1 Talk about these questions. Find the words in *italics* in your
   dictionary. They are all in the story.
   a Would you like to live on a *farm* on a small *island*? Why (not)?
   b Where do you find *rocks, cliffs, waves* and *sandbanks*?
   c If you are *alone*, is anybody with you?
   d When do you call an *ambulance* in an *emergency*?
   e In a *storm*, what flies through the *air*?
   f Why are there a lot of bad *stepmothers* in stories?
   g What do the *engine* and the *wheel* do on a boat?
   h What can you do with a *rope*?
   i Think of a problem in your life now. Is it your *fault*?
   j When can you see the *moon*?
   k Why do people wear *life jackets*?

After you read

2 Answer these questions.
   a Why doesn't Tessa like her stepmother, Sheena?
   b Why does she want to work in Inverkeld?
3 Read the names of Chapters 1–4 again, and tell the story.
   Chapter 1   A Girl Alone
   Chapter 2   Emergency!
   Chapter 3   Into the Storm
   Chapter 4   The Lights of Inverkeld

Chapters 5–8

Before you read

4 Tessa and Jim are on a sandbank. What are they going to do now?
   Will they get to Inverkeld? What do you think?
5 How do *coastguards* save *lives*? Find the words in *italics* in your
   dictionary and answer the question.

25

After you read

6 Who says these words. Who are they talking to?

    a 'We can only wait.'

    b '*You* can't climb.'

    c 'Send somebody quickly, please.'

    d 'That's not possible!'

    e 'You came back!'

    f 'He's yours, too.'

7 Discuss the end of the story. Is Tessa's life going to change now? How?

Writing

8 You are Tessa. On the day before the storm, write a letter to a friend in Inverkeld. Write about your life on the island. How do you feel? What do you really want to do?

9 Write a letter to the same friend a week after the storm. How do you feel now? How is your life different?

10 You are Sheena. Write a letter to your mother the day after the storm. Tell her about your new baby, and about your feelings for Tessa.

11 You work for a newspaper, the *Inverkeld Times*. Write the story of Tessa and Jim on the night of the storm.

Answers for the Activities in this book are published in our free resource packs for teachers, the Penguin Readers Factsheets, or available on a separate sheet. Please write to your local Pearson Education office or to: Marketing Department, Penguin Longman Publishing, 5 Bentinck Street, London W1M 5RN.